HOLIDAY TIME

Look for these
and other books
in
The Kids in Ms. Colman's Class series

#1 *Teacher's Pet*
#2 *Author Day*
#3 *Class Play*
#4 *Second Grade Baby*
#5 *Snow War*
#6 *Twin Trouble*
#7 *Science Fair*
#8 *Summer School*
#9 *Halloween Parade*
#10 *Holiday Time*
#11 *Spelling Bee*

Jannie, Bobby, Tammy, Sara
Ian, Leslie, Hank, Terri, Pamela
Nancy, Omar, Audrey, Chris, Ms. Colman
Karen, Hannie, Ricky, Natalie

THE KIDS IN
MS. COLMAN'S CLASS

HOLIDAY
TIME
Ann M. Martin

Illustrations by Charles Tang

A
LITTLE APPLE
PAPERBACK

SCHOLASTIC INC.
New York Toronto London Auckland Sydney

No part of this publication may be reproduced in whole or in part, or stored in a retrieval system, or transmitted in any form or by any means, electronic, mechanical, photocopying, recording, or otherwise, without written permission of the publisher. For information regarding permission, write to Scholastic Inc., Attention: Permissions Department, 555 Broadway, New York, NY 10012.

ISBN 0-590-06003-1

12 11 10 9 8 7 6 5 4 3 2 1   7 8 9/9 0 1 2/0

Printed in the U.S.A.   40
First Scholastic printing, November 1997

The author gratefully acknowledges
Gabrielle Charbonnet
for her help
with this book.

FIRST SNOWFALL

"Ugh," said Sara Ford's mother. She was scraping snow off of the windshield of the car.

"Isn't it pretty?" Sara asked. Their front yard was covered with a velvety layer of clean snow. The bushes looked like giant cotton balls. The lawn looked like a soft flannel blanket. Sara loved snow.

"Ugh," said Mrs. Ford again. "Yes, it is pretty. As long as it is not on my car."

Soon the windshield was clean. Sara climbed into the front seat.

"It is almost December," said Sara. "You know what that means."

Mrs. Ford smiled and started the car.

1

"Um, six more months till summer vacation?" she guessed.

"No!" said Sara. "It means my two favorite holidays are coming up."

"Valentine's Day and St. Patrick's Day?"

"Mommy!" Sara knew her mother was just kidding. "I mean Christmas and Kwanzaa."

"Ohhhh," said Mrs. Ford. "Yes, those are nice holidays. Do you remember the year your father knocked over the Christmas tree?"

Sara laughed. "Yes."

Sara and her mother talked about Christmas and Kwanzaa all the way to Stoneybrook Academy.

"And here we are at school," said Mrs. Ford. "Do you have your lunch?"

"Yes." Sara kissed her mother goodbye and ran through the gate to the playground. This was her first year at Stoneybrook Academy. So far Sara liked her new school. The other kids were pretty

2

nice, and Audrey Green was Sara's good friend. Best of all was her second-grade teacher, Ms. Colman, who was really, really, really nice.

"Hey, Sara!" called Audrey. "Do you want to help me make snowcats?"

Sara smiled. Audrey was under the big oak tree. She was scooping up snow and patting it into small cat figures around the base of the tree.

"Okay," said Sara. "Maybe I will make a snowdog, like Frederick." Frederick was Sara's family's dachshund. They had bought him several months earlier. Sara began to pat snow into a long hot-dog shape.

By the time the bell rang, Sara had finished her dachshund. Audrey had made several more snowcats.

"We can make even more at lunchtime," said Audrey as they hurried to Ms. Colman's class.

"Okay," said Sara.

Inside the classroom, Sara hung her coat in her cubby and sat down at her desk.

The other kids came in, laughing and stamping snow off of their boots. There were six boys and ten girls. The boys were Ian Johnson, Bobby Gianelli (Bobby was the meanest boy in class), Hank Reubens, Chris Lamar, Ricky Torres, and Omar Harris.

The girls were Jannie Gilbert and Leslie Morris, who were best friends, Audrey (of course), Natalie Springer (who everyone thought was the class baby), Tammy and Terri Barkan, who were twins, and Karen Brewer, Hannie Papadakis, and Nancy Dawes, who were best friends. Sara was the tenth girl.

Karen was going to have a sleepover the weekend after next. Every girl in the class was invited. Sara had received her invitation the day before. She could hardly wait.

Soon Ms. Colman arrived. Small snowflakes stuck to her dark, curly hair. She smiled at everyone. Sara smiled back. When Ms. Colman smiled, she looked as if she really meant it.

"Our first snowfall!" said Ms. Colman. Sara could tell that Ms. Colman liked snow as much as Sara did. "As soon as I take attendance, we will talk about the first snowfall and what it means. Then I will make an announcement."

"Oh, boy," said Karen. Sara could see her wiggle in her seat. (Karen sat in the front row, because she wore glasses. Ricky and Natalie also wore glasses and sat in the front row.)

Sara felt excited. Ms. Colman's announcements were almost always something good.

THREE SPECIAL
HOLIDAYs

"Soon it will be December," said Ms. Colman, once she had taken attendance. "In December three important holidays take place. Does everyone know what they are?"

"Christmas!" Karen shouted.

"Indoor voice, Karen," said Ms. Colman. "And please raise your hand next time."

"Sorry," said Karen.

Sara raised her hand. "Kwanzaa," she said.

"That is right," said Ms. Colman. "And one more."

"Hanukkah," said Nancy.

"Very good," said Ms. Colman. "Hanukkah, Kwanzaa, and Christmas are three important holidays. Today we are starting a new unit about those holidays. We will learn about their history, their traditions, and their songs. We will even learn about the special decorations and foods that people use in their celebrations."

"Cool," whispered Ian. He sat next to Sara.

"Then," continued Ms. Colman, "before our winter vacation, we will have a class party. We will celebrate the holidays together."

"Yea!" everyone shouted.

Sara turned to look at Audrey. Audrey smiled and gave Sara a thumbs-up. The unit on holidays sounded like a lot of fun.

"Now, I have divided the class into three groups," said Ms. Colman. "Each group will research one holiday. In three weeks we will have class presentations. Over several days, each group will give reports about its holiday's traditions, customs, songs, and food."

Ms. Colman read her lists. In the Christmas group were Karen, Leslie, Natalie, Omar, and Hank. In the Hanukkah group were Audrey, Hannie, Bobby, Ricky, and Terri. In the Kwanzaa group were Sara, Tammy, Chris, Ian, Nancy, and Jannie.

Sara was happy to be in the Kwanzaa group. She already knew a lot about Kwanzaa, because her family celebrated it every year. It would be fun to teach her classmates about it.

"Excuse me, Ms. Colman?" said Nancy. "Shouldn't I be in the Hanukkah group? I am Jewish and we celebrate Hanukkah."

Ms. Colman smiled. "Our new unit will teach all of us about all of the holidays," she said. "It does not matter if you are Christian or Jewish or white or black. We are going to learn about different holidays together. We will see that these holidays have some things in common, as well as some things that are different. Okay?"

"Okay," said Nancy.

"Good. Now let's split up into our groups," said Ms. Colman. "You may start talking about your holidays."

At lunchtime Sara and Audrey found two seats together in the lunchroom. Sara pulled out her lunch. She had brought a thermos of tomato soup, a cheese sandwich, carrot sticks in a baggie, and two cookies. She ate the cookies first.

"What are you going to do for the Hanukkah project?" asked Sara.

Audrey took a sip of milk. "Food," she said. "Hanukkah has all sorts of special foods. My job is to make something and bring it to school. Then we will all share it at our holiday party."

"Great!" said Sara. "My job is food too — Kwanzaa food. I am going to make something delicious."

Audrey smiled. "What will it be?"

"I do not know yet," said Sara. "I will have to ask my mommy."

"Me too," said Audrey.

3

WHICH RECIPE?

That weekend Sara told her parents about Ms. Colman's unit on holidays.

"I have to make a special Kwanzaa dish and bring it to school," said Sara.

"I guess Ms. Colman does not know you cannot cook to save your life," said Marcus. Marcus was Sara's nine-year-old brother.

"That is enough, Marcus," said Mrs. Ford. She turned to Sara. "I think it is a lovely idea. What are you planning to make?"

"I do not know," said Sara. "Will you help me decide?"

"Sure," said Mrs. Ford. "We can look

through our Kwanzaa cookbooks after dinner."

"How about a nice sweet-potato casserole?" said Mr. Ford. "Those are always good."

"Um, maybe," said Sara. "I will have to see."

After dinner Sara and her mother sat at the kitchen table. They looked through several cookbooks. Frederick came in and sat under their feet.

"How about this?" said Mrs. Ford. "It is a good vegetable dish."

Sara looked at the recipe. It had many ingredients. She would have to cut and chop and mix a lot of things. She would have to use a food processor, which she could not do by herself. She would have to fry things on top of the stove, which she could not do by herself.

"It looks yummy," said Sara. "But I do not want a lot of help. I want to be able to do most of it myself. It is my project."

"Oh, I see," said her mother. "Let's keep looking, then."

Sara looked at many recipes. Many seemed too difficult. Some sounded as if they would not taste very good.

Then Sara saw a cookie recipe. It did not seem too difficult. It was for sugar cookies with sesame seeds. Sesame seeds are important in traditional African cooking. And the cookies would be nice to have at Ms. Colman's holiday party.

COOK BOOK

"This is it!" Sara said. "This is the one. I can do all of it myself, except turn on the oven and take the cookies out afterward. Will you help me with just those things?"

"I would be happy to," said Mrs. Ford. "We will write down the ingredients you need. Then you can make a practice batch of cookies."

"Great!" said Sara. "These cookies will be perfect!"

4

A NEW STUDENT

"Guess what," said Audrey on Monday.

"What?" said Sara.

"Karen and Nancy are having a big fight," said Audrey. "Nancy says that Karen did not invite her to the sleepover. Karen says she did. She thinks Nancy's invitation got lost in the mail. So now they are not speaking. And I heard Karen uninvite Nancy to the sleepover."

"Wow," said Sara. "That is serious. It is too bad they are fighting. They are best friends. With Hannie, they are the Three Musketeers." That was what Karen, Nancy, and Hannie called themselves.

"Yes, and now Nancy is the only girl in our class who will not be at the sleepover," said Audrey. "I feel bad for her."

"Me too," said Sara. "Friends should not have fights."

"Nope," agreed Audrey. "Anyway, what have you decided on for your holiday food?"

"Sesame-seed cookies," said Sara. "I only need a tiny bit of help to make them. What are you going to make?"

"Noodle kugel," said Audrey. "It is very good. I love noodle kugel. It is like a cross between pudding and a pie. But you make it with noodles. And it is very easy. You just throw it together."

Sara smiled at Audrey. She wondered how Audrey's noodle kugel would turn out. Sometimes Audrey was accident-prone. Sara hoped nothing would go wrong with Audrey's recipe.

A few days later Ms. Colman made another one of her announcements. After

Ricky had taken attendance, Ms. Colman said, "Today a new student is going to join our class. I hope you will make her feel — "

The classroom door opened then, and a tall, pretty girl came in by herself. She looked around at all the students. Sara's eyes widened. On Sara's first day at Stoneybrook Academy, her mother had brought her to the classroom. Sara had felt so shy that she had not been able to look at anyone. This new girl did not look shy at all.

"Boys and girls," said Ms. Colman, "this is Pamela Harding. Karen, would you please show Pamela where our cubbies are?"

Karen led Pamela to the wall of cubbies. Pamela hung her coat in an empty cubby. Beneath her coat she was wearing a very cool outfit — the kind of outfit Sara would love to wear but was afraid to try. Pamela had on pink overalls, a striped pink-and-white shirt, pink high-top sneakers, and a hat. Sara wondered what *she*

would look like in that outfit. She sighed. She would probably not look as cool as Pamela did. Pamela looked like a third-grader, at least. Maybe even a fourth-grader. Sara was short and looked younger than her age.

Ms. Colman asked Pamela to introduce herself, and Pamela told the class about her family. Her mother was a writer, her father was a dentist, and she had a sixteen-year-old sister. Her sister let Pamela use her perfume. Sara sighed again. Dumb old Marcus, she thought. He was just a *brother.* He was only nine years old. He would not be caught dead wearing perfume. He was not good for very much, Sara decided. She would trade him in a second for a sixteen-year-old sister who would let Sara try her perfume.

"And Pamela will be in the Christmas group," Ms. Colman said. "Leslie, will you explain our holiday unit to Pamela later? Right now it is time for spelling."

Pamela sat at Ms. Colman's desk until

21

the school custodian brought her a desk and chair of her own. Pamela did not seem to mind that everyone was looking at her.

I wish I were like Pamela, thought Sara. Cool as a cucumber.

THE COOKIE FAILURE

That night Sara decided to make a practice batch of cookies. Then she would know exactly how to make the cookies for the holiday party. There would be no surprises.

The recipe listed all the ingredients she would need: flour, sugar, vanilla extract, butter, eggs, baking powder, sesame seeds, salt.

"Salt?" asked Sara. "In cookies?"

"Yes," said Mrs. Ford. "Should I stay and help you? Do you understand everything you need to do?"

"No, and yes," said Sara. "I will call you when it is time to put the cookies in the oven."

"Okay," said Mrs. Ford. She turned on the oven to let it preheat. Then she left Sara in the kitchen.

Marcus came in from the family room. "I hope your teacher knows you are going to poison everyone," he said. He took an apple from the fruit basket and bit into it. "I am glad I do not have to eat your cookies."

"Oh, be quiet," said Sara. "You will see. My cookies will be so delicious that you will beg me to have one. And I will say no."

Marcus laughed. "I do not think so."

"Mommy!" Sara called. "Marcus is bothering me. I am trying to do my school project. He is in the way."

"Okay, okay," said Marcus. "Go on and make your poison cookies. I am leaving."

The recipe said to cream the butter and the sugar together. Sara put them in a bowl and stirred and stirred until her arms felt like limp noodles. Then she added the flour and stirred some more. Then she added the rest of the ingredients. The batter smelled so good that Sara ate a tiny bit of it. Finally she spooned the batter onto a cookie sheet. She made neat rows of dough lumps. She sprinkled the dough lumps with sesame seeds.

"Mommy!" she called. "I am ready for you to put the cookies in the oven!"

Mrs. Ford came into the kitchen. "They look very good, Sara," she said. "They look just as they should. Now we will bake them for nine minutes." She put the cookies in the oven and set the timer.

Sara sat down to wait. It was the longest nine minutes of her life.

Ding! went the timer.

"Mommy!" Sara called, but Mrs. Ford was already walking into the kitchen.

"Mmm, smells good in here," she said. She picked up a pot holder. "Let's see your beautiful cookies."

Sara waited impatiently while her mother took the cookie sheet out of the oven.

"Hmm," said Mrs. Ford.

Sara leaned over eagerly to see her neat rows of cookies. Then she frowned. "What happened?" she said. "That is not my batch of cookies."

On the cookie sheet, instead of several rows of cookies was just one big, flat cookie. It filled the sheet. The edges were burned dark brown. The middle looked wet and unbaked.

"Did you put in all the ingredients?" asked Mrs. Ford.

"Yes," said Sara.

"It looks like you used baking soda instead of baking powder," said Mrs. Ford.

"Is there a difference?" asked Sara.

"Oh, yes," said Mrs. Ford. "When they say *powder* they really mean it."

"Oh." Sara was very disappointed. She had thought making cookies would be a snap. But her first batch was a failure. There was no way she could bring this monster cookie to class. What would Pamela Harding think?

"Why don't you make another batch?" suggested Mrs. Ford. "Just pay close attention to the recipe. I am sure your second batch will be fine."

"Okay," said Sara. She rolled up her sleeves and got ready to beat more sugar and butter together.

6

THE EXPLODING KUGEL

"Exploded?" asked Sara at school the next day. "How could a kugel explode?"

"I do not know," said Audrey sadly. Audrey was giving Sara a progress report on her Hanukkah recipe. It had not gone well. "I followed the recipe exactly. Then I decided to use the microwave instead of the regular oven, because I am allowed to turn on the microwave. But the kugel just exploded! It made a big mess, and I had to clean it up. By myself."

"I know what you mean," said Sara. "My cookies did not turn out well either.

The first batch turned into one horrible monster cookie. The second batch did not flatten out. They baked into hard little lumps. And my third batch looked very pretty but tasted awful. I do not know why. I made them the same way every time."

"Did you ask your mommy to help you?" asked Audrey.

"No. But after the third batch she said maybe I did need help. She said she did not want me to waste any more food, even though I was not doing it on purpose." Sara stamped the snow beneath her feet. "I think maybe I will find another recipe."

"Good idea," said Audrey. "That is what I am going to do too. Do not worry. I am sure we will both come up with yummy dishes."

Sara smiled at Audrey. "I am sure you are right."

"Can you come to my sleepover to-morrow night?" Karen asked Pamela. It was lunchtime, and the girls in Ms. Colman's class had surrounded Pamela at a lunch table. Most of the girls had, anyway. Sara noticed that Natalie, Tammy, and Nancy were sitting at another table. Audrey was still in the lunch line, but Sara had saved her a place.

Pamela took another bite of her sandwich. "I guess so," she answered.

"Great!" Karen exclaimed.

Audrey sat down next to Sara.

"Pamela is coming to my sleepover tomorrow night," Karen told Audrey. "We will have so much fun. No party poopers allowed."

Sara thought that was a mean thing to say about Nancy.

"I got out my sleeping bag last night," said Audrey. "Do I need to bring anything else?"

"Just your nightgown and a toothbrush," Karen said. "Hey, Pamela, do you want to play foursquare? The snow has melted from the blacktop."

Pamela sighed. "I guess," she said.

Karen, Pamela, Hannie, and Leslie ran outside to play.

"Let's hurry and finish our lunches," said Sara. "Then we can get in line to play foursquare."

"Do you like foursquare?" Audrey asked. "You have never played it before."

"Sometimes I play," said Sara. "I want to see if Pamela is a good player."

Audrey wrinkled her nose. "Pamela is not very friendly," she said. "I have tried to talk to her a couple times, and she acts as if I am a big baby or something."

"No she doesn't," said Sara. "Pamela is very cool. She wears great clothes."

"That does not make her a nice person," said Audrey.

"Pamela is fine," said Sara. "She just has to get used to us. Are you done with lunch?"

"Yes. But I do not want to play foursquare. I think I will go to the library instead."

Sara shrugged. "Okay. See you later."

* * *

On the playground, Sara got in line behind Ricky Torres.

"We put up our Christmas tree last week," Ricky was telling Ian. "On December first. It practically touches our ceiling."

"I am going to help my dad put up our Christmas lights this weekend," said Ian. "Our house will look so cool."

In the foursquare game, Bobby knocked Pamela out. She frowned and went to the back of the line, next to Sara.

Sara gave her a big smile, but Pamela did not smile back.

"I am going to the mall this weekend," said Sara. "I will have my picture taken with Santa."

"We are going to go on Saturday," said Ricky. "Maybe I will see you there."

"Are you going to have your picture taken with Santa?" Sara asked Pamela.

Pamela looked at her. "I have never had my picture taken with Santa," she said. "He is not even the real Santa, you know."

"I know that," said Sara. "He is just Santa's helper. But it is fun to have your picture taken with him."

"It is for babies," said Pamela.

Sara had not thought of it that way. Was Pamela right?

KAREN'S SLEEPOVER

"I am not sure I want to do this," said Sara.

She and her mother were waiting in line to have Sara's picture taken with Santa.

"Why not?" asked her mother.

Sara looked at the line of kids waiting. Many of them were much younger than her. Some were actually babies. But some kids were older than Sara too. Sara was not sure what to think. She had asked Audrey about it. Audrey did not think it was baby-ish.

"Pamela thinks it is for babies," Sara had told Audrey.

"Pamela is silly."

Sara did not think that Pamela was silly. She thought Pamela was great.

"It is almost our turn, sweetie," said Mrs. Ford. "I think it would be nice to have your picture taken with Santa. But it is your decision."

Sara looked at Santa. She decided she was too old to have her picture taken with him.

"I do not want to," she told her mother.

"Oh. Well, that is too bad," said Mrs. Ford. "I like looking at all of your Santa pictures. But you can always change your mind before Christmas, if you want."

"Now, let's go to the bookstore," said her mother. "We can look at some Kwanzaa cookbooks. Maybe we will find a better recipe for you to try."

That afternoon Mr. Ford dropped Sara off at Karen's father's house. (Karen lived at two houses: her mother's house and her father's house. That was because her parents were divorced.) Karen's father's house was very, very big.

"Hi, Sara," said Karen. "Thank you for coming. We are all in the playroom."

Karen's playroom was decorated with balloons and crepe-paper streamers. It looked very partyish. Jannie, Leslie, Hannie, Pamela, Natalie, and Audrey were already there. They had spread their sleeping bags out on the floor. Sara spread hers out next to Audrey's.

"Pamela does not have a sleeping bag," Audrey told her. "She only sleeps in beds." Audrey rolled her eyes.

Sara did not think that was so strange. It sounded kind of cool. She almost wished she had not brought her own sleeping bag.

Karen's sleepover was a lot of fun. The girls ate pizza on the floor in the playroom, like a picnic.

"We do not have a playroom," said Pamela. "We have a *den*."

Sara thought *den* sounded much more grown-up than *playroom.* At her house they called it a family room. She could not tell if that sounded babyish or not.

After dinner they watched *The Wizard of Oz.* Sara thought it was scary. She could tell that Pamela did not.

"Aiiee!" Audrey screamed when the flying monkeys grabbed the scarecrow. She held on to Sara's arm.

Sara gently pushed Audrey's hand

away. Pamela was smirking at Audrey. "It is just a movie, Audrey," Sara said.

Audrey looked at her in surprise.

The rest of the sleepover was very exciting. The girls made Slice 'n Bake cookies. (They got into a food fight. Well, everyone except Pamela did.) Karen and Nancy made up over the phone, and Nancy came to the party. Then Charlie (one of Karen's older stepbrothers) told a spooky story. There was a big thunderstorm, and the

electricity went out. Then the lights came back on again.

It was very, very late when everyone finally climbed into their sleeping bags and went to sleep. (Pamela went to Karen's room and slept in her bed.)

The next day everyone's parents picked them up. After Pamela left, Audrey said, "I do not think she had a very good time."

"I do not think *she* is very much fun," said Hannie.

"She was a party pooper," said Nancy.

"She does not count," said Karen. "Forget about her."

Sara frowned. Pamela seemed so cool and grown-up. Why were the other girls picking on her?

OKRA IS MAJORLY YUCKY

"Ew," said Sara. Carefully she cut another piece of okra.

After school on Tuesday, she had started making her new recipe: stewed okra. Okra is a vegetable. It is about as big as a man's thumb, and is filled with small seeds. Her mother made it sometimes, and Sara knew it was yummy.

Mrs. Ford had given Sara a knife that was not too sharp, but sharp enough to cut okra. After cutting up the okra, Sara was going to mix it with a can of tomatoes and the other ingredients, then microwave everything.

"Ew," Sara said again. She did not remember okra looking like this. Every time she cut it, long, stringy strands of goo stretched between the pieces. It was disgusting.

Mrs. Ford came into the kitchen. "Everything going okay?"

"Is it supposed to look like this?" asked Sara, wrinkling her nose.

Her mother glanced at the pile of cut okra. "Uh-huh. That looks fine."

"Okaaaay." Sara took a deep breath and began cutting again. Her hands were getting sticky. The cutting board was sticky. Her knife was sticky. Maybe something was wrong with the okra.

"Ew, disgusting," said Marcus, peeking over Sara's shoulder.

"Mommy!" called Sara. "Marcus is bothering me!"

Marcus picked up a piece of okra. He

pretended to sneeze loudly into his hand. "Oh, excuse me!" he said, stretching long okra strings between his fingers. (Sara's stomach felt funny.)

Finally all the okra had been cut up. It was oozing in a pile on the cutting board. Sara tried not to look at it. She put tomatoes, onions, and spices into a microwave-safe mixing bowl. She scraped the okra into it. The cutting board looked like a bunch of slugs had held a party on it.

Then she microwaved everything.

When Sara took out the bowl, it smelled okay. And it looked okay, until she stirred it. Then she saw the long, stretchy strings. Her mother had said they would go away as the okra cooked. But they had not. Suddenly Sara felt that she could not look at the casserole for one more second. It was completely gross. No way would the kids in Ms. Colman's class eat it. Pamela Harding would take one look at it and say, "Ew. Gross."

Sara began to scrape it into the disposal. Then she remembered what her mother had said about the cookies. She had said that Sara was wasting food. Was Sara wasting all this okra? Probably.

"What can I do?" Sara whispered to herself. "I cannot eat this. I cannot ask my friends to eat it. But I do not want to waste food either."

The kitchen door pushed open, and Frederick wiggled his long body through the opening. He snuffled at Sara's feet in a friendly way, then went to his dish to see if he had food. He did not. He had already eaten his breakfast, and it was not dinnertime yet.

Ah. "Here you go, boy," said Sara. She scraped the okra casserole into Frederick's bowl. "Try this. If you eat it, it will not be wasted."

Frederick sniffed the mess in his bowl. He licked the edge.

"Is it too spicy?" asked Sara. "Just give it a try. I bet you will like it."

Frederick looked at Sara, then wagged his tail. He bent his head and took a small bite of okra. He began to eat the casserole. Sara watched him. He liked it!

"Good boy, Frederick," she said.

PAMELA: YES OR NO?

When Sara arrived at school on Monday, Audrey was not making snowcats under the oak tree. She was swinging slowly.

"Hi," said Sara. "What are you doing?"

"I am listening to everyone," said Audrey. She pointed at Karen, Hannie, and Nancy. They were playing hopscotch.

"*They* have all decided they do not like Pamela," said Audrey. "They are against her. But look at Jannie and Leslie and Terri."

Jannie, Leslie, and Terri were sitting at Pamela's feet. Pamela was sitting on a big tree root. She was talking and waving her hands. Jannie and Leslie and Terri were laughing.

"They are for Pamela," said Audrey. "And there are Natalie and Tammy." She pointed to where they were playing foursquare with Ian and Chris. "Natalie and Tammy are not for Pamela or against her."

"Why would anyone be against Pamela?" asked Sara. She sat down in a swing next to Audrey. "She wears the coolest clothes. She acts so grown-up. She knows about all kinds of things."

"But is she nice?" asked Audrey. "Is she friendly?"

"She is being friendly to Leslie, Jannie, and Terri," Sara pointed out. "And she has been nice to me."

Actually, Sara could not remember a specific nice thing that Pamela had done. But that was because Pamela had just started school. Sara was sure that once Pamela got to know everyone better, she would seem nicer and friendlier.

"So you are for Pamela," said Audrey.

Sara frowned. "There is nothing wrong with Pamela."

"If you say so," said Audrey. "Hey, how did your latest recipe turn out?"

Sara was glad to talk about something besides Pamela. She groaned loudly to show Audrey how bad her okra casserole had been. "It was awful," she said. "I did not even finish it. I have to find a new recipe."

"Me too," said Audrey with a smile. "I tried making matzo balls. They are dumplings made of special flour. My mommy makes them to put in chicken soup. They are usually very soft and light, like feathers."

"The ones you made were not light?" asked Sara.

"Well, my daddy is using one as a paperweight for his desk now. What does that tell you?" Audrey kicked her shoe against the rubber blacktop under the swing.

"Not light," said Sara.

"Right," said Audrey.

* * *

After lunch Ms. Colman asked the class to separate into their holiday groups. The Kwanzaa group met in the corner by the windows.

"I have been thinking," said Sara. "There are six of us in our group. And there are seven days of Kwanzaa. Each day has a special meaning. We can each represent a day. Someone will have to be two days."

"We can make decorations too. And

wear traditional African costumes," said Jannie.

"My mommy can help us," said Sara. "She knows all about stuff like that."

Just then, loud voices across the room interrupted them.

"You be quiet, Pamela!" Karen was yelling.

Pamela giggled. "You are mad because you are such a baby," she said. "You and your baby Christmas elf."

"I am not a baby!" Karen said, putting her hands on her hips. "And the Christmas elf is fun. My family has been doing the Christmas elf ever since I was born."

"Maybe it is time to move on," said Pamela.

Karen took a step forward. For a moment it looked as if she might slap Pamela. But Ms. Colman was too quick for her.

"Girls, please," said Ms. Colman. "You do not seem to be showing much holiday spirit. I would like you to apologize to each other. Then try to work together peacefully in your group."

"I am sorry," Pamela said cheerfully.

Karen glared at her. Then she muttered, "I am sorry." She did not sound as if she meant it.

Sara turned back to her own group. She wished everyone would try harder to make Pamela feel welcome.

10

No Pickled Herring

"Hmm," said Mrs. Ford.

"Maybe I forgot to put in the water," said Sara.

Sara's Liberian rice bread looked more like a brick than a loaf of bread. It was solid and very heavy, although it had *sounded* easy to make. Sara had mixed the ingredients together, and her mother had put the pan in the oven.

"I do not think we can eat this," said Mrs. Ford.

"I guess not," Sara said. She felt very discouraged. She had tried several recipes now, and none of them had turned out well.

"Are you going to try it again?" asked her mother.

Sara shook her head. "I will do something else. I do not know what. But I will think of something."

After Mrs. Ford left the kitchen, Sara broke off the hard, dry crust. She scooped out the doughy inside and called Frederick. Although he coughed once or twice, he was able to get most of the bread down.

At least it is not being wasted, Sara thought.

"I wonder if Frederick feels all right," said Mrs. Ford.

"Why?" asked Mr. Ford. "Is something wrong with him? Marcus, could you please pass the rolls?"

"Here," said Marcus, handing his father the basket of rolls. "These are safe to eat. Sara did not make them."

"That is enough, Marcus," said Mrs.

Ford. "I am worried about Frederick because he has not been eating very much lately."

Sara stopped in mid-chew.

"No?" said Mr. Ford. "I give him breakfast every morning. He always looks happy to get it."

"He does eat breakfast," said Mrs. Ford. "But he has not eaten his dinner in days."

Mr. Ford glanced at Frederick, sleeping on the floor. "He does not look any skinnier," he said. "In fact, he looks fatter."

"It is very strange," said Mrs. Ford. "I hope he is okay."

"We will keep an eye on him," said Mr. Ford. "Could you please pass the meat loaf, Marcus?"

Sara looked down at her plate. She knew why Frederick was not eating his dinner.

Later that week Sara went to Audrey's house after school. Audrey had not had success with any of her recipes either. The girls had decided to team up. Maybe together they could create the perfect dish.

"Have you ever had pickled herring?" asked Sara.

"No," said Audrey. "It is preserved fish. Like sardines. My parents eat it. And my brother, Abram, eats it too, when he is home." Audrey's older brother was away at college.

"Okay, well, let's try it," said Sara.

The recipe was simple, and the girls did not have to cook anything. Together they carefully double-checked the ingredients, then mixed them in a bowl. Audrey dumped the pickling mixture over the small fish fillets.

"The recipe says to wait for two weeks," said Audrey. "But we do not have that much time. We have to present our food next Friday."

"Maybe we should just taste it now," said Sara.

Each girl took a tiny bite of pickled herring.

Sara made a face. "This cannot be people food."

Audrey shook her head. "I know we did everything correctly," she said. "But there is something wrong. This is just too yucky."

"Maybe penguins would like this," said Sara, giggling.

Audrey laughed too. "Or maybe it is just for grown-ups. Or snobs, like Pamela Harding."

Sara quit giggling. "Pamela is not a snob."

"Oh, sure she is," said Audrey. "She is always bragging about something. It is always her mother this, her sister that. All she talks about is how much better her old house was, and her old school. Haven't you heard her?"

Sara had not had much chance to talk to Pamela. Pamela was always surrounded by Jannie and Leslie and sometimes Terri. But Sara felt sure that Pamela was not a snob.

"I wish you would quit picking on her," said Sara. She felt a little angry.

Audrey looked surprised. "I am not picking on her. It is a fact: Pamela is a snob. And she can be mean sometimes too. I heard her tell Natalie to wear tights instead of socks. Because tights cannot fall down."

"Well, Natalie's socks *are* always falling down," said Sara.

"I know, but it is not nice to tease her about it," said Audrey.

"You are just jealous," Sara blurted out.

Audrey's eyes widened. "Jealous?"

"Yes," said Sara. She was about to say something mean, but she could not stop herself. "You are jealous because Pamela is pretty and wears great clothes. And she is grown-up and cool."

Audrey glared at Sara. "So you are saying I am an uncool baby."

"Well, you said it. Not me." Sara felt terrible as soon as the words came out of her mouth.

Audrey stared at Sara. Her lower lip quivered. Just then they heard the doorbell ring.

"That is your mommy, coming to pick you up," said Audrey. "And I am glad. I want you to go home."

Sara was already sorry about what she had said, but she could not say so. Instead she said, "Me too."

WHAT TO DO?

The next day, after lunch, Ms. Colman asked her class to form their holiday groups.

It was hard for Sara to pay attention. Audrey was not speaking to her. Sara had eaten lunch with Tammy Barkan. She had wanted to sit at Pamela's table, but there were no free seats.

Now the kids in her group were talking about their Kwanzaa presentations.

"I have bought seven candles," said Chris. "Three red ones, one black one, and three green ones. Nancy and I can tell the class what each candle stands for during Kwanzaa."

"You know what," said Nancy. "Hanukkah uses special candles also. But they can be all different colors."

"I have made the special Kwanzaa table mat," said Tammy. "I am going to tell everyone how to make one, and why people use them at Kwanzaa."

"We are going to have the best presentations ever," said Nancy. "Sara, how is your special Kwanzaa food coming along?"

Sara jumped. She had not been listening until Nancy asked her about the food. What could she say? The presentations were to begin the next day. The food was needed on Friday. She had only three days left.

"Oh, it is fine," she said. "No problem. It will be very delicious."

"What are you making?" asked Ian.

"Um . . . it is a surprise," said Sara. "But it will be very good, you will see."

Nancy smiled. "Natalie is making special Christmas cookies," she said. "But Audrey is having a hard time finding the right recipe. Audrey said she might just buy store-made macaroons."

Sara felt sad that Nancy knew Audrey's plans and she did not. That is what happens when friends fight.

"Pamela, you are not singing the right tune," said Karen loudly from across the room.

Everyone in class turned to look at the Christmas group.

"Me?" said Pamela. "You are the one who sounds like a frog. A sick frog."

"There they go again," said Jannie. "Karen keeps asking for trouble. Pamela says that anyone so full of hot air ought to be used as a Thanksgiving Day balloon."

That did not sound like a very nice thing for Pamela to say, thought Sara. On the other hand, Karen *was* a blabbermouth.

"Pamela is the one full of hot air," Nancy said to Jannie. "Karen is standing up for herself."

"You are just saying that because

Karen is your best friend," said Jannie. "But Pamela is right."

Sara sighed and put her head in her hands. First she and Audrey. Now Nancy and Jannie. Everyone in class was arguing — all because of Pamela. But it was not Pamela's fault, was it?

12

POOR FREDERICK

That afternoon Sara checked on her black-eyed-pea soup. She had made it in her mother's Crock-Pot. (Sara was allowed to use the Crock-Pot by herself.) She took out a long spoon and ate a couple of black-eyed peas. They crunched between her teeth. When Grammy Ford made them, they were smooth and soft and chewy. Not crunchy.

Sara swallowed hard. She drank a glass of water. "Frederick!" she called.

"Oh my goodness," said Mrs. Ford a little while later.

Sara was in her room, doing her

spelling homework. She had missed two words on her last spelling quiz. Now she was writing them each ten times, very neatly.

"What is the matter?" Sara heard Marcus ask their mother.

"Frederick has been sick," said Mrs. Ford. "Could you please bring me a roll of paper towels?"

"Oh, yuck," said Marcus. "He barfed?"

Sara bit her lip. Frederick *had* eaten a lot of black-eyed peas. But he seemed to enjoy them. They could not have made him sick, could they?

Sara went out into the hall. Her mother was cleaning the floor with disinfectant. Frederick was sitting nearby, looking embarrassed.

"Frederick was sick?" Sara asked.

"Yes," said her mother. "Not just here, but in the family room also. It is very weird. I do not know what he has been eating. It almost looks like . . ."

Mrs. Ford straightened up. She looked

at Sara. Then she looked at Frederick. "Sara, weren't you making black-eyed peas in the Crock-Pot?"

Sara gazed at her feet.

"What happened to them, honey?" asked her mother. "Where did you put them? Could Frederick have gotten to them?"

"Um," said Sara.

"Sara?"

"Well, I . . ."

Mrs. Ford gathered her cleaning supplies and stood up. "Please come with me, Sara. We need to talk."

"I did not mean to make Frederick sick," Sara said, sniffling. Her mother handed her a tissue.

"Have you been feeding Frederick all of your recipes?" asked Mrs. Ford.

Sara nodded. "You said the cookies were wasted food, since we could not eat them. But Frederick will eat almost anything. I thought giving him the food was better than wasting it."

"So this is why Frederick has been getting fatter and fatter without eating his dinner," said Mrs. Ford.

"Uh-huh."

"I guess the black-eyed peas were the last straw. Now his tummy is upset. What was wrong with the peas?"

"They were crunchy," said Sara.

"Okay. Listen," said her mother. "Frederick is just a little dog. He does not know what is best for him."

Across the room, Frederick thumped his tail.

"That is why we have to take good care of him," Mrs. Ford went on. "Taking care of him means making sure he eats good dog food, and not a lot of people food. Also, not too *much* food. From now on, you must not give him anything to eat without checking with me or your daddy first. Okay?"

"What about dog treats?" asked Sara.

"Two dog biscuits in the morning, two liver snacks at night," said Mrs. Ford. "No more."

"Okay," said Sara.

"And now that Frederick is overweight, he will need more exercise until he slims down. It will be your job to take him for extra walks. Every day after school, you must walk him around the block four times."

"Okay." Walking Frederick around the block four times would take forever. Frederick always stopped about a million times. He had to sniff everything.

"Now, what are you going to make for your Kwanzaa dish?" asked her mother.

"I do not know," said Sara unhappily. "I just do not know."

HOLIDAY PRESENTATIONS

On Tuesday afternoon the holiday presentations began. First Chris held up a black candle in front of everyone in Ms. Colman's class. He put it in the special Kwanzaa candleholder, called a *kinara*.

"On the first day of Kwanzaa," he said, "people light the black candle. The black candle stands for *umoja*, which is a Swahili word meaning unity."

Nancy stepped forward. She held up a red candle, then placed it in the *kinara* next to the black candle.

"On the second day of Kwanzaa," she

71

said, "a red candle is lit. It stands for" — Nancy read carefully from an index card — "*kujichagulia.* That means self-determination. And that means learning about African traditions. Or practicing traditions you already know."

Chris and Nancy took turns talking about the seven days of Kwanzaa and putting candles into the *kinara.* Chris talked about *ujima,* working together. Nancy talked about *ujamaa,* putting everyone's money together for one purpose. Chris talked about *nia,* which means purpose or goal. Nancy held up a red candle for *kuumba,* creativity. They explained the last candle, a green one, together.

"*Imani* means faith," said Chris.

"Faith means you expect good things in the future," said Nancy.

The class clapped when they were finished.

Ms. Colman said, "Very well done, Chris and Nancy."

Next, Ricky and Hannie showed

everyone how to play the dreidel game for Hanukkah. They explained about Hanukkah *gelt*.

"Excellent," said Ms. Colman when they were finished.

The last presentation of the day was by the Christmas group. Ms. Colman had said that Karen and Pamela had to work together. So the two of them stood in front of the class and talked about Christmas spirit. Karen was wearing red jeans and a green sweatshirt. Pamela was wearing black velvet overalls, a thermal-weave turtleneck, and a gold Leo zodiac charm on a black silk cord. She looked almost like a fourth-grader.

"Christmas spirit is not something you can see or taste or hear," said Karen. She looked stiff and angry, standing next to Pamela. "It means feeling love and kindness toward everybody. It means forgiving everyone and hoping nice things happen to them."

Sara thought that Karen did not look

like she wanted anything nice to happen to Pamela.

Pamela stepped forward. "Christmas spirit means enjoying giving presents to people, and doing nice things for them. Especially if you do them secretly. Almost like you were a Christmas elf." Pamela put her hand over her mouth and giggled.

Karen gasped and whirled on Pamela. "Pamela!" she cried. "Quit making fun of my family's Christmas elf!"

Pamela just giggled harder.

Hmm, thought Sara. It was not very nice of Pamela to tease Karen about her family's tradition. Especially in front of the whole class. Even though having a Christmas elf did sound a little babyish. Sara wondered if Karen had had her picture taken with Santa this year.

"Girls," said Ms. Colman. Ms. Colman hardly ever raised her voice, but Sara could tell she was not happy with Karen and Pamela. "You two are not a good example of the Christmas spirit. I am not very pleased with this presentation."

Karen looked as if she were about to say something, but she did not. She just stomped back to her desk and sat down. Pamela sat down at her desk.

I have only three days left, thought Sara. She wondered if Audrey really was going to *buy* macaroons. She missed Audrey.

"Audrey, could you please erase the board for me before our social-studies lesson?" asked Ms. Colman.

Audrey stood up. Sara saw that one of her shoes was untied. Before Sara could warn her, Audrey stepped on the laces and tripped. She fell on her stomach on the floor. In front of everyone.

But Ms. Colman's class seemed to have some Christmas spirit. No one laughed or pointed. Tammy helped Audrey to her feet.

"Audrey, are you all right?" asked Ms. Colman.

"I am okay," Audrey said. Her face was red with embarrassment. Sara wanted to say something nice to make Audrey feel better, but she was sitting too far away. Also, she and Audrey were not speaking.

Then Sara heard Pamela say, "Oops. There she goes again."

Jannie and Leslie smiled.

"She must have tripped on a Christmas elf," whispered Pamela.

"BE QUIET!" Karen yelled.

"Pamela, Karen, that is quite enough," said Ms. Colman firmly. "I will speak to you both after class."

At that moment Sara made up her mind about Pamela. She was not trying very hard to be friendly.

You might *look* nice, Pamela, Sara thought. But you are actually *not* very nice. And Audrey is. I will remember that.

BINGO

That afternoon Sara's mother gave Sara permission to walk down the street to Audrey's house.

Audrey looked surprised to see Sara at her door.

"I came to say I am sorry," said Sara quickly. Apologizing was like taking off a Band-Aid. It hurt less if you did it fast, all at once. "I was wrong about Pamela. I am sorry she was mean to you today. And I did not mean what I said the other day. I take it back."

"You said I was babyish," Audrey reminded her.

"You are not any more babyish than I am," said Sara.

Audrey thought for a moment. "I forgive you."

"Thank you," said Sara. "So we are not fighting anymore?"

Audrey smiled. "I guess not."

"Good," said Sara. "Because I really need help."

"What about this one?" said Audrey. She took a sip of chocolate milk.

Sara and Audrey were sitting at Audrey's kitchen table. Every cookbook in the house was spread open on the table.

Sara ate a cookie. "It looks too difficult. See, your mommy would have to fry the onions."

They had been looking at recipes for almost an hour. Not one seemed just right, for either Hanukkah or Kwanzaa.

"What are we going to do?" wailed Audrey. "I need a Hanukkah recipe. You need a Kwanzaa recipe. And we need them by Friday!"

"Maybe we should ask our parents to make things for us," said Sara.

"Well, we *could*," said Audrey. "That does not seem like much fun, though."

"Natalie is making special Christmas cookies," said Sara. "She has been talking about them. She has Christmas cookie cutters. Her parents bought her all kinds of icing and sprinkles and stuff."

"Oh, no." Audrey moaned. "Her cookies will be great. And what do I have? An exploding kugel, matzo balls you could use as doorstops, and disgusting pickled fish."

Sara laughed. "I made one humongous cookie, a loaf of bread that could break a window, and some awful, crunchy black-eyed peas that made Frederick sick."

Audrey looked at Sara. Sara looked at Audrey. Now they both were laughing.

"I am glad we are friends again," said Sara.

"Me too," said Audrey.

They began looking through the cookbooks once more.

"Yum," said Audrey. "Potato latkes. I love those."

"What are they?" asked Sara.

"They are also called potato pancakes," said Audrey, "but they are not really like pancakes. They are more like french fries, but all lumped up. They are delicious."

"Are they hard to make?" asked Sara.

Audrey read the recipe. "Not really. You just grate up some potatoes and a little onion. Then you add some flour and salt and pepper. But then you have to fry them."

"Hmm," said Sara. "They sound good. We could ask your mommy or daddy to fry them for us, after we make them."

"Wait, wait!" said Audrey. "Here is a recipe for *baking* the latkes. That way Mommy would only have to open the oven for me, instead of frying and frying and frying." Audrey looked at Sara. "I think this is it!"

"It might be it for *you*," said Sara sadly. "But my Kwanzaa dish is still missing."

"Could we say they are Kwanzaa latkes?" asked Audrey.

Sara shook her head. "I do not think so. Besides, we eat mostly sweet potatoes during Kwanzaa. Not white potatoes."

"Could you make sweet potato latkes?" asked Audrey.

"I guess," said Sara. "But they would still be latkes. You have given me an idea, though. My daddy said he always liked sweet-potato casserole. I had not thought of it before. But I wonder if I could make one."

"Let's look for a recipe," said Audrey.

A few minutes later they found it.

"Look," said Sara. "You take sweet potatoes, oranges, and chopped-up peanuts. Then you put in brown sugar and salt and apple juice. It sounds yummy."

"It sounds different," said Audrey. "At my house we usually make sweet potatoes with little marshmallows on top."

"I do not think marshmallows are very African," said Sara. "But this recipe sounds good. Mommy would have to bake it for me. She might even have to help with cutting up the sweet potatoes. But that is okay."

"Yes," said Audrey. "Isn't there a

Kwanzaa day when everyone works together?"

"The third day," said Sara. "*Ujima*. That is right — I had not thought of that. You and I working together to find a recipe is like *ujima*. And Mommy helping me make my recipe is also like *ujima*. That makes it even more Kwanzaa-ish."

Sara and Audrey smiled at each other. Then they slapped high fives. Their holiday presentations were saved!

A HOLIDAY SUCCESS

"Today is the last day before our winter vacation," said Ms. Colman on Friday. "To end our unit on holidays, each group will present its special holiday songs. Afterward, we will have our class party. Now we will start with the Hanukkah group."

Audrey, Hannie, Bobby, Ricky, and Terri stood at the front of the class. They sang "Dreidel, Dreidel, Dreidel," "Hanukkah, O Hanukkah," and "The Blessing for the Candles."

Everyone clapped when they were done.

"Very nice, Hanukkah group," said Ms. Colman. "We have all learned a lot about Hanukkah, the Festival of Lights, this past week, and why it is a very special holiday. Thank you."

Everyone clapped again.

"Now it is the Christmas group's turn," said Ms. Colman.

Karen, Leslie, Natalie, Pamela, Omar, and Hank came to the front of the room. They sang "O Christmas Tree," "Silent Night," and "Santa Claus Is Coming to Town." Karen and Pamela managed to

make it through their songs without getting into a fight.

"That was very nice," said Ms. Colman. "Your group had some lovely presentations also." She did not say, *Except for the one about Christmas spirit*. But Sara thought that's what everyone was thinking.

Next was the Kwanzaa group. First they sang "The Kwanzaa Song." Then Sara and Tammy played some traditional African drums that Mr. Ford had lent them.

Then the group showed the class a dance they had been rehearsing.

By the time her group was finished, Sara felt full of holiday happiness. The presentations had gone very well, and her group had taught the class about Kwanzaa. Not only that, but she and Audrey had made up. And they had each found a holiday recipe that worked! Things could not get better. Even Frederick was looking and feeling better again.

"And now what you have all been waiting for," said Ms. Colman. "It is time for our holiday food presentations and our class party."

"Yea!" everyone cried.

Natalie's Christmas cookies were a big hit. She had decorated them to look like Christmas trees, bells, holly leaves, wrapped packages, and even snowmen and reindeer.

On the party table Audrey placed a platter of potato latkes, with applesauce and sour cream.

Next to it was Sara's sweet-potato casserole. Mrs. Ford had put it in her electric casserole dish, so it would stay warm.

There were also cupcakes, punch, and peppermint sticks.

"You know what?" Sara said to Audrey once they had filled their paper plates.

"What?" said Audrey. She used a peppermint stick to stir her punch.

"We have learned all about holiday traditions," said Sara. "But I know what the best holiday tradition is: friendship."

"You are one hundred percent right," said Audrey. And she and Sara laughed.

It was going to be a wonderful holiday.

L. GODWIN

About the Author

ANN M. MARTIN lives in New York and loves animals, especially cats. She has two cats of her own, Gussie and Woody.

Other books by Ann M. Martin that you might enjoy are *Rachel Parker, Kindergarten Show-Off* and the Baby-sitters Club series. She has also written the Baby-sitters Little Sister series starring Karen Brewer, one of the kids in Ms. Colman's class.

Ann grew up in Princeton, New Jersey, where she had many wonderful teachers like Ms. Colman. Ann likes ice cream, *I Love Lucy*, and especially sewing.

THE KIDS
IN
MS. COLMAN'S CLASS

A new series by Ann M. Martin

Don't miss #11
SPELLING BEE

"I have an announcement," said Karen.

"No, *we* have an announcement," said Hannie Papadakis. Hannie, Nancy, Audrey, and Sara were standing next to Karen.

"Okay, *we* do," said Karen.

"So what is your big announcement?" asked Chris.

"A *girl* is going to win our class spelling bee," replied Karen.

"No, *Karen* is going to win it," said Audrey.

By now everyone was looking at Karen. And all the girls were crowded behind her.

"Girls are smarter than boys!" shouted Pamela.

Little Sister

by Ann M. Martin
author of The Baby-sitters Club®

❑	MQ44300-3	#1	Karen's Witch	$2.95
❑	MQ44259-7	#2	Karen's Roller Skates	$2.95
❑	MQ44299-7	#3	Karen's Worst Day	$2.95
❑	MQ44264-3	#4	Karen's Kittycat Club	$2.95
❑	MQ44258-9	#5	Karen's School Picture	$2.95
❑	MQ44298-8	#6	Karen's Little Sister	$2.95
❑	MQ44257-0	#7	Karen's Birthday	$2.95
❑	MQ42670-2	#8	Karen's Haircut	$2.95
❑	MQ43652-X	#9	Karen's Sleepover	$2.95
❑	MQ43651-1	#10	Karen's Grandmothers	$2.95
❑	MQ43645-7	#15	Karen's in Love	$2.95
❑	MQ44823-4	#20	Karen's Carnival	$2.95
❑	MQ44824-2	#21	Karen's New Teacher	$2.95
❑	MQ44833-1	#22	Karen's Little Witch	$2.95
❑	MQ44832-3	#23	Karen's Doll	$2.95
❑	MQ44859-5	#24	Karen's School Trip	$2.95
❑	MQ44831-5	#25	Karen's Pen Pal	$2.95
❑	MQ44830-7	#26	Karen's Ducklings	$2.95
❑	MQ44829-3	#27	Karen's Big Joke	$2.95
❑	MQ44828-5	#28	Karen's Tea Party	$2.95
❑	MQ44825-0	#29	Karen's Cartwheel	$2.75
❑	MQ45645-8	#30	Karen's Kittens	$2.95
❑	MQ45646-6	#31	Karen's Bully	$2.95
❑	MQ45647-4	#32	Karen's Pumpkin Patch	$2.95
❑	MQ45648-2	#33	Karen's Secret	$2.95
❑	MQ45650-4	#34	Karen's Snow Day	$2.95
❑	MQ45652-0	#35	Karen's Doll Hospital	$2.95
❑	MQ45651-2	#36	Karen's New Friend	$2.95
❑	MQ45653-9	#37	Karen's Tuba	$2.95
❑	MQ45655-5	#38	Karen's Big Lie	$2.95
❑	MQ45654-7	#39	Karen's Wedding	$2.95
❑	MQ47040-X	#40	Karen's Newspaper	$2.95
❑	MQ47041-8	#41	Karen's School	$2.95
❑	MQ47042-6	#42	Karen's Pizza Party	$2.95
❑	MQ46912-6	#43	Karen's Toothache	$2.95
❑	MQ47043-4	#44	Karen's Big Weekend	$2.95
❑	MQ47044-2	#45	Karen's Twin	$2.95
❑	MQ47045-0	#46	Karen's Baby-sitter	$2.95
❑	MQ46913-4	#47	Karen's Kite	$2.95
❑	MQ47046-9	#48	Karen's Two Families	$2.95
❑	MQ47047-7	#49	Karen's Stepmother	$2.95
❑	MQ47048-5	#50	Karen's Lucky Penny	$2.95
❑	MQ48229-7	#51	Karen's Big Top	$2.95
❑	MQ48299-8	#52	Karen's Mermaid	$2.95
❑	MQ48300-5	#53	Karen's School Bus	$2.95
❑	MQ48301-3	#54	Karen's Candy	$2.95
❑	MQ48230-0	#55	Karen's Magician	$2.95
❑	MQ48302-1	#56	Karen's Ice Skates	$2.95
❑	MQ48303-X	#57	Karen's School Mystery	$2.95
❑	MQ48304-8	#58	Karen's Ski Trip	$2.95

More Titles... ➡

♥ ♥

The Baby-sitters Little Sister titles continued...

❑	MQ48231-9	#59	Karen's Leprechaun	$2.95
❑	MQ48305-6	#60	Karen's Pony	$2.95
❑	MQ48306-4	#61	Karen's Tattletale	$2.95
❑	MQ48307-2	#62	Karen's New Bike	$2.95
❑	MQ25996-2	#63	Karen's Movie	$2.95
❑	MQ25997-0	#64	Karen's Lemonade Stand	$2.95
❑	MQ25998-9	#65	Karen's Toys	$2.95
❑	MQ26279-3	#66	Karen's Monsters	$2.95
❑	MQ26024-3	#67	Karen's Turkey Day	$2.95
❑	MQ26025-1	#68	Karen's Angel	$2.95
❑	MQ26193-2	#69	Karen's Big Sister	$2.95
❑	MQ26280-7	#70	Karen's Grandad	$2.95
❑	MQ26194-0	#71	Karen's Island Adventure	$2.95
❑	MQ26195-9	#72	Karen's New Puppy	$2.95
❑	MQ26301-3	#73	Karen's Dinosaur	$2.95
❑	MQ26214-7	#74	Karen's Softball Mystery	$2.95
❑	MQ69183-X	#75	Karen's County Fair	$2.95
❑	MQ69184-8	#76	Karen's Magic Garden	$2.95
❑	MQ69185-6	#77	Karen's School Surprise	$2.99
❑	MQ69186-4	#78	Karen's Half Birthday	$2.99
❑	MQ69187-2	#79	Karen's Big Fight	$2.99
❑	MQ69188-0	#80	Karen's Christmas Tree	$2.99
❑	MQ69189-9	#81	Karen's Accident	$2.99
❑	MQ69190-2	#82	Karen's Secret Valentine	$3.50
❑	MQ69191-0	#83	Karen's Bunny	$3.50
❑	MQ69192-9	#84	Karen's Big Job	$3.50
❑	MQ69193-7	#85	Karen's Treasure	$3.50
❑	MQ69194-5	#86	Karen's Telephone Trouble	$3.50
❑	MQ06585-8	#87	Karen's Pony Camp	$3.50
❑	MQ06586-6	#88	Karen's Puppet Show	$3.50
❑	MQ06587-4	#89	Karen's Unicorn	$3.50
❑	MQ06588-2	#90	Karen's Haunted House	$3.50
❑	MQ55407-7		BSLS Jump Rope Pack	$5.99
❑	MQ73914-X		BSLS Playground Games Pack	$5.99
❑	MQ89735-7		BSLS Photo Scrapbook Book and Camera Pack	$9.99
❑	MQ47677-7		BSLS School Scrapbook	$2.95
❑	MQ43647-3		Karen's Wish Super Special #1	$3.25
❑	MQ44834-X		Karen's Plane Trip Super Special #2	$3.25
❑	MQ44827-7		Karen's Mystery Super Special #3	$3.25
❑	MQ45644-X		Karen, Hannie, and Nancy	
			The Three Musketeers Super Special #4	$2.95
❑	MQ45649-0		Karen's Baby Super Special #5	$3.50
❑	MQ46911-8		Karen's Campout Super Special #6	$3.25

Available wherever you buy books, or use this order form.

Scholastic Inc., P.O. Box 7502, Jefferson City, MO 65102

Please send me the books I have checked above. I am enclosing $_____
(please add $2.00 to cover shipping and handling). Send check or money order – no
cash or C.O.Ds please.

Name_____Birthdate_____

Address_____

City_____State/Zip_____

Please allow four to six weeks for delivery. Offer good in U.S.A. only. Sorry, mail orders are not
available to residents to Canada. Prices subject to change.   BSLS497

♥ ♥

The Adventures of THE BAILEY SCHOOL KIDS ®

Creepy, weird, wacky and funny things happen to the Bailey School Kids!™ Collect and read them all!